by Michael Scotto
cover art by Evette Gabriel
chapter art by Dion Williams
edited by Ashley Mortimer
typography by Kevin Dinello
© National Network of Digital Schools 2010

By Michael Scotto

Sensei's Garden

With Illustrations By
Evette Gabriel & Dion Williams

little
lincoln

Contents

CHAPTER 1

Sensei's Advice

Midlandia was an island of great beauty. For a place so small, it had a wide variety of landforms. There were plains with tall grass and a valley with green hills. A mountain range stood on one edge of the island. A large forest with hiking trails lined the other end.

The forest trails had become Deja and Logan's favorite place to visit. Logan loved to take pictures of the forest with his new digital camera. Deja liked to make funny poses in the pictures.

Or at least she usually did. Today, Deja did not seem very eager.

"No, no, bend your elbow more!" Logan told Deja, aiming the camera lens.

Deja bent her elbow a few inches. She was standing next to a young tree that was about her height. The tree had a branch that looked like a waving arm. Logan was trying to make Deja pose exactly like the tree.

"How's this?" asked Deja, her voice dull.

Logan lowered his camera and let it hang from the strap around his neck. "Is something wrong?" he asked.

"I don't know," Deja said with a sigh.

"It seems like something's wrong to me," replied Logan. He took his glasses from his shirt pocket and put them on. "I can't remember the last time I saw you without a smile on your face. A big, sunny, silver smile."

That did make Deja grin a little. Deja wore braces, and they shined like polished silver whenever she smiled.

"What's going on today?" Logan asked her.

"Well... there is something," Deja said. "You know how I like to figure things out?"

Logan nodded. He knew all about Deja's favorite hobby. She was a very curious girl who enjoyed learning how different machines worked. She found out how they worked by taking them apart and rebuilding them. Deja's father had even gotten her a toolbox with her name stenciled on the side.

"I saw my dad's old radio in the barn this weekend," Deja said. "And I got really curious about it."

Logan had a feeling that he knew what Deja was going to tell him.

"It was pretty easy to take apart," Deja went on. "But there were so many parts inside! A lot more than I thought there would be."

"And you can't figure out how to put it back together," guessed Logan.

"Yeah," Deja said. "I hid the radio under my bed. But my dad listens to it whenever he's working on the farm. He even asked me if I knew where it was this morning!"

"Did you tell him?" asked Logan.

"Heck, no!" Deja said, shaking her head. The beads at the ends of her braided hair clinked together. "He's going to be so mad at me. I don't know what to do."

Logan wasn't sure what she should do either. But he had an idea of who might know.

"We could talk to Sensei," he suggested.

"You think?" replied Deja.

"His garden is at the top of the trail," Logan said. "Let's go."

Sensei was a wise, older Midlandian who was well-known for his good advice. Midlandians of all ages, from Dewey the librarian to Coach O. Bobo, came to him for help with their problems. Even Chief Tatupu, the leader of Midlandia, sometimes came to him for answers.

Sensei spent most of his time taking care of

his garden. He called the garden his sanctuary. Logan and Deja were not sure exactly what that word meant, but they knew that Sensei's garden was the place where he always felt his best.

After a short hike, Deja and Logan had reached the garden. The stone walls of the garden were draped with vines and lilacs. There were hundreds of colorful flowers growing in the dirt.

"Greetings, children!" Sensei said with a wave. "Have you come to help me with my new project?"

Sensei was hard at work right near one of the garden walls. He was digging a deep pit in the soil.

"Actually, we came to get some advice," Deja told him.

"That is most unusual," said Sensei, leaning on his shovel.

"What's weird about asking for help?" inquired Logan.

"Nothing at all," Sensei replied. "It is good to ask a friend for help when one cannot find the answers. I just mean that usually, it is you and your friends who are helping us Midlandians, not the other way around."

The kids could see Sensei's point. Logan, Deja, and their friends had helped the Midlandians many times in the past.

Logan and Deja were part of a group of eight

special students called the Kid Council. The Kid Council's job was to help the citizens of Midlandia with their daily problems. The Kid Council members took turns traveling to Midlandia to help out and solve mysteries.

"I'll tell you what," said Sensei. "Grab some shovels and gardening gloves. You can help me dig while you share your troubles."

As the three worked together, Deja explained her radio problem.

"When my dad finds out that I messed with his radio," she said, "he'll ground me 'til I'm in high school!"

"It is true that you should have asked first if you wanted to learn about his radio," said Sensei. "But if you are honest, I do not think your father will overreact. Perhaps you can work with him to put the radio back together."

"Maybe you're right," Deja replied. "My dad does like to do projects with me."

Sensei nodded. "As the Midlandian poet Whitman Wannadogood once wrote, '*I only speak with most sincerity. It leaves my soul in sweet serenity.*'"

Sensei noticed the puzzled looks on the children's faces. "That is a fancy way to say that being honest makes you feel good inside," he explained.

"Ah, that makes sense," stated Deja.

"When I give advice," Sensei continued, "I like to use poems to show my point. I have gained a lot of wisdom from poetry."

"Thanks for the advice, Sensei," Deja said.

"And thank you for helping me dig this hole," Sensei replied. "It is almost deep enough."

"What's the hole for?" asked Logan.

"I am installing a small pond with a little waterfall in it," Sensei explained. "It will be perfectly peaceful."

"We're happy to help!" Deja said, as she plunged her shovel into the ground.

"Ouch!" she hollered.

Sensei became concerned. "Oh, no! Did you get a splinter from the shovel's handle?" he asked.

"No," Deja replied. "I just hit something very hard in the ground. It shook my arms."

"You must have hit a rock," Logan concluded.

Sensei poked his shovel in the dirt and it made a loud clanging noise. "It seems that you are right, Logan," he said. "We'll need to dig around it and remove it."

Sensei, Deja, and Logan all dug around the edge of the rock. Once it was free, Sensei lifted it from the ground.

"What in the name of Midlandia?" said Sensei. He brushed dirt off of the large object.

"What's the matter?" asked Deja.

"I don't think this is a rock at all," replied Sensei. "I think it's a bone!"

CHAPTER 2

A Dirty Discovery

After Sensei and the kids discovered the strange object in the garden soil, Sensei called in the experts.

Antigua was an archaeologist. Her friend and partner, Venture, was an anthropologist. They both studied people, animals, places, and objects from the past. They were professors at the University of Midlandia.

Deja and Logan had been watching the pair work for an hour. At the moment, Venture was holding the mystery object up with a pair of metal tongs. Antigua was studying its details with a very large magnifying glass.

Finally, Antigua lowered her magnifying glass. "This is definitely a bone of some kind," she said to Venture.

"But what sort of bone?" wondered Venture. "And from what creature?"

"All I can say for sure is that it came from something large," replied Antigua.

Venture paced back and forth in front of Deja and Logan. They were sitting near the hole in Sensei's garden.

"So many questions!" Venture cried. "So much to discover!"

"You sure seem excited," Deja told him.

"You bet I'm excited!" Venture replied. "This discovery could be huge. No, more than huge—it could be monumental! Just think of the possibilities! We could write a book! Become famous!"

"Venture," Antigua cut in, "before we plan our world tour, I'd like to send you on an important mission."

"A mission?" Venture asked eagerly. "I'm on it!"

Antigua pulled an instant camera from her knapsack. She took a few quick pictures of the bone Sensei had found.

"Take these to the Midlandia Library," Antigua instructed. She handed the pictures to Venture. "See if you can find any pictures of a skeleton that has this bone. Pay special attention to the spinal column."

Venture nodded sharply. He hopped on his bike and raced toward town.

"There!" said Antigua. "Venture is a great partner, but he can become a little too excitable for my tastes."

Logan politely raised his hand. "May I take a couple of pictures with my camera, too?" he asked.

"Of course," Antigua replied.

"Cool!" Logan said. He began to click photos of the scene.

Deja raised her hand. She had a question for Antigua, too.

Antigua smiled. "You know," she said, "you don't have to raise your hand to ask me questions. What's up?"

"What's a spiral column?" asked Deja.

"I think you mean *spinal* column," Antigua replied. "That is another term for your backbone. Did you know that your backbone is actually made up of more than one bone? It's a whole series of bones. It protects your spinal cord and helps you to stand up straight. Your skull sits right on top of it."

"Oh!" Deja said. "Well, do you think the bone we found is part of a... spinal column?"

"I can't be sure, of course," said Antigua. "But, I have seen many a skeleton in my day. This bone looks similar to many vertebrae that I have studied. Vertebrae are what you call the bones in the spinal column. Humans have many of them."

"So I have a backbone, and this animal has a

backbone, too," Deja said. "That's pretty cool!"

"It is cool," Antigua agreed.

Logan returned to Antigua and Deja. "I got some great pictures of the bone we found," he said. "Antigua, do you think there are more bones like this around here?"

"That is an excellent question," said Antigua. "And my answer is, yes."

"Wow!" Deja exclaimed. "Sensei, did you hear that?"

Deja turned around. "Sensei?" she called out.

Sensei had disappeared!

"Where'd Sensei go?" asked Deja.

"I think he went to the meadow," answered Logan. "He said he wanted to... meadow-tate, or something."

Antigua chuckled. "I believe he went to meditate," she said. "That means that he went to sit quietly and think."

"You sure know a lot of words," Logan told her.

Antigua grinned. "I thought I saw Sensei go inside his gardening shed," she said.

Antigua and the kids opened the door to the gardening shed. There they found Sensei sitting on the shed floor. His eyes were closed. He was very still.

"Is he asleep?" Logan whispered.

"I am not asleep," said Sensei, opening his eyes. "I was just deep in thought."

"Guess what, Sensei?" asked Deja. "Antigua thinks there are more bones in your garden!"

"That is very interesting!" Sensei replied.

"There's just one thing," said Antigua. "The only way I'll know for sure is if I keep digging."

Sensei became concerned again. "Would your work interrupt my gardening?" he asked.

For the first time today, Antigua did not seem to have an answer ready. "I'm afraid so," she finally said. "Venture and I would have a lot of digging to do. It could take a great deal of time."

Sensei did not respond.

"We'll be very careful around your plants," Antigua promised. "We'll try to dig up as few plants as possible. When we are finished, we will put everything back in place."

Sensei thought about what Antigua was saying. "How old do you think that bone is?" he asked.

"I can't be sure until we test it," she replied. "But it could be thousands of years old. Maybe millions! If that is true, then Venture would be right—it would be an important discovery."

"It could go in the museum!" added Logan.

"I would hate to get in the way of a great discovery," said Sensei.

"Would you be willing to let Venture and me take over your garden for a while?" asked Antigua.

Sensei nodded his head, though he seemed reluctant to do so. "I will miss my garden," he said. "But there are plenty of other fun places for me to spend my time... right?"

"You could take an art class," Logan suggested.

"Or you could go to the dentist!" Deja said.

"He said 'fun places,' Deja," replied Logan.

"What? I like the dentist!" Deja said.

"Now, now, let's not argue," said Sensei. "Everything will work out. After all, in the words of Byron O. Bobo, the famed Bobolian poet, '*A sudden turn can be a fright, but sometimes, change leads to delight.*'"

CHAPTER 3

The Angry Visitor

Not long after their talk with Antigua, Deja and
Logan returned home for the weekend. On Monday
morning, they were back in Midlandia.

"Do you think Antigua found any more bones
in Sensei's garden?" Logan asked Deja.

"We should go find out," Deja replied. "I need
to talk to Sensei anyway."

"Oh," Logan said. "Do you need more advice?"

"Nope!" Deja said proudly. "I just want to
thank him. I told my dad the truth about how I

took his radio apart. Dad was upset at first, but then we worked to put the radio back together. It works fine now, and I got to do a cool project with my dad!"

The two friends hiked the trails to Sensei's garden. When they arrived, the garden looked very different from the last time they had seen it.

Where green grass and colorful flowers had once grown, the kids now saw nothing but a large, deep hole in the ground.

"All of the plants have been dug up!" Logan said to Deja.

"Not all of them!" called a voice from inside the deep hole.

It was Antigua. She popped her head up out of the hole. She pointed to the corner of the garden. "I left a shrubbery over there," she said. "It is untouched."

"Where's Sensei?" asked Deja.

Antigua climbed a stepladder and hopped out of the hole. "He's been gone all weekend," she said. "I think it made Sensei sad to see his garden like this. We had to dig up a lot more than I first thought."

Venture's head popped up into view. "A small price to pay, I say!" he declared. "It's a small price to pay for fame, fortune, and glory!" He ducked back down and returned to digging.

"Do you really think that what we found will make us famous?" asked Logan.

"Venture is getting a little bit ahead of himself," Antigua replied. "His search in the library did not give us much information. We still don't even know exactly what kind of animal these bones came from."

"Bones?" Logan repeated. "You found more of them?"

Antigua broke into a proud grin. "We did!" she said. "Come look."

Antigua led Deja and Logan over to a big cloth that was spread on the ground. There were several bones lined up on the cloth. They all looked similar.

"These are more back and neck bones," Antigua explained.

"Wow, our animal had a long neck," Logan noticed. "Maybe it was a giraffe!"

"I don't think so," said Antigua. "These bones are millions of years old. Also, they are hollow."

"Hollow bones?" asked Logan.

"That's right. Once we cleaned the bones up and studied them, we realized that they used to be empty inside," said Antigua. "Giraffes do not have hollow bones."

Antigua noticed that Deja had been very quiet

this whole time. She did not seem interested in the bones. "Is everything quite all right, Deja?" she asked.

Deja nodded. "I'm fine," she said. "I'm just worried about Sensei, I guess. I hope he's not too sad about his garden being all dug up."

Antigua nodded her head. "If you're worried about Sensei, you should go talk to Chief Tatupu," she said. "Sensei and Chief are very close."

"Thanks!" Deja said. She and Logan headed for the town square.

Chief Tatupu was the leader of Midlandia. He had an office in the Community Center in Midlandia's town square. From there, Chief helped Midlandians with their daily problems and listened to their complaints.

When Deja and Logan got to Chief's office door, someone was complaining very loudly.

"He's a menace!" the voice cried. "A menace, I tell you!"

"Now, now," Chief replied. "There is no need to exaggerate."

"Who is that?" Logan asked Deja.

"I think it's Brushy," she replied. She peeked around the doorframe into Chief's office.

Deja was right. Brushy, the town dentist, was red in the face from his yelling.

"Could you please start at the beginning?" Chief asked Brushy.

"Okay, I'll try," Brushy said. "It all started at the end of last week when Sensei came to visit me for a checkup."

"I guess Sensei took your advice," Logan whispered to Deja.

"His teeth were fine," Brushy continued. "It was obvious that he brushes and flosses very well. But after I told Sensei he was free to go, well... he didn't leave!"

"He did not leave?" asked Chief.

"He stayed and watched my next five appointments—as if he had nothing better to do!" Brushy exclaimed. "What's worse, he kept giving me advice on how to do my job! 'Hold the mirror here, Brushy. You'll see better with more light, Brushy.'"

"That is most unusual," Chief commented.

"The next day, it was the same thing!" Brushy went on. "I was so bothered that I canceled my afternoon appointments. I decided to go to the zoo to relax."

"I am glad that you found a solution that did not involve fighting," Chief said.

Brushy held up his hands. "I'm not finished yet, Chief," he said. "I went to Animal Land. I was there to pursue my hobby of bird-watching. Birds are such fantastic creatures. They are perfect little flying machines. They even have hollow bones to make them lighter."

Logan's eyes lit up as he listened. "Did you hear that?" he whispered to Deja. "Birds have hollow bones, just like the bones we found in the garden!"

Brushy continued talking in Chief's office. "I was on the lookout for one of my favorite birds— the golden pheasant! It has golden feathers on its crown and near the tail. It has stripes along its neck. Its wings are bold blue!"

"Yes, yes, but what happened?" asked Chief. He knew that Brushy could flap his beak about birds for days on end.

"Well, after only three hours, I caught sight of the bird with my binoculars!" Brushy said. "I grabbed my camera to take a picture. But just before I could get a snap of the pheasant's majestic mantle—"

"Sensei came by again," Chief guessed.

Brushy nodded with a frown. "He came in and asked me if I needed any help," he grumbled. "I said no, but instead of leaving, he sat down and told me a poem about birds. He scared off the pheasant with his noise and my picture was ruined!"

"I am sorry to hear that," Chief said.

"And then..." Brushy began. "Then I sort of lost my temper, I'm sorry to say."

"I will have a talk with Sensei about his behavior," Chief said. "Thank you for coming in."

Brushy stood and straightened his lab coat. "No, no, thank you, Chief," he said. "The next time you want your teeth cleaned, it's on the house!"

"Um, great!" replied Chief. He walked Brushy to the door. As Brushy left, Chief spotted Deja and Logan, who were sitting as quietly as fallen leaves.

"Have you two been here this whole time?" asked Chief.

"We wanted to ask if you could help us find Sensei," Deja explained.

"We can look for him together," suggested Chief, and off the trio went.

CHAPTER 4

Unwanted Help

Chief led Deja and Logan down the road toward Animal Land. He thought that Sensei might still be there.

"I can't wait to take all sorts of pictures of the animals," Logan said. "Maybe I'll even see the golden pheasant that Brushy was looking for."

"It is fine to take some pictures," Chief said. "But remember, we are looking for Sensei. He needs our help."

"I know, Chief," replied Logan.

Deja walked along quietly. "Chief?" she said. "I feel sort of guilty."

Chief looked over at her in surprise. "What is wrong?" he asked.

"This whole thing is my fault," Deja said. "I was the one who found that bone in the first place. I hit it with my shovel when we were digging. If it wasn't for me, Sensei's garden would be just fine and he wouldn't be acting weird."

Chief put a hand on Deja's shoulder. "You

should not feel guilty," he told her. "This situation is no one's fault."

"Why do you think Sensei was pestering Brushy?" asked Logan.

"We will figure that out as soon as we find Sensei," Chief replied.

After a short while, Chief and the kids reached Animal Land.

Animal Land, Midlandia's zoo, was divided into many different areas. Each area was made to look and feel like a different kind of environment. This way, each animal had a home that was like its natural habitat.

In the middle of it all stood a building called the conservation center. That was where Wilda, the zookeeper, had her office. She also had a small hospital there for sick and hurt animals.

"We will search more quickly if we split up," Chief said. "If anyone finds Sensei, bring him to the conservation center. We can all meet there."

Everyone went a separate way. Logan decided to search the desert area first. He saw many critters and cacti on the sandy ground, but no Sensei.

Meanwhile, Deja had decided to search the rainforest area of Animal Land. She saw tall trees and swinging monkeys, but Sensei was not there, either.

Chief started at the far end of the zoo. The area was made to look like a deciduous forest. He peeked around every oak and elm tree, but Sensei was nowhere to be found.

Chief did see something he recognized, though. "The golden pheasant!" he said. The colorful bird was walking near a huckleberry bush. "I wish I had Logan's camera!"

Deja, Logan, and Chief kept searching through the grasslands, the wetlands, and every kind of land between.

Soon the trio had searched the whole zoo without luck. They all met outside of the conservation center.

"Perhaps Wilda has seen Sensei," Chief said. "We can find her in here."

Chief and the kids entered the conservation center. They saw a door with a red first aid symbol on it. "This leads to the animal hospital," Chief explained.

Logan could hear voices from inside the hospital area. "It sounds like Wilda is in there," he said. "Let's knock first."

Chief knocked on the hospital door. He and the kids heard footsteps approach, and then Wilda opened the door.

"Chief!" she said. "How nice to see you."

"I hope that we are not bothering you," Chief said. "We are looking for Sensei."

"You've come to the right place," Wilda told him. "He's right here in the hospital."

"Oh, no!" Deja gasped. "Is he hurt?"

"No, no, no," Wilda said. "My only patient right now is a baby alligator with an injured foot. I'm taking care of him and Sensei is... helping me, I guess."

Wilda invited her visitors inside. Logan spotted Sensei on the other side of the room. He was standing near the baby alligator's bed. There was a lamp above the bed to keep the alligator warm.

Sensei smiled when he saw Deja and Logan. "Hello, young ones!" he said.

"How are you, Sensei?" asked Logan.

"I don't miss my garden, that's for sure," said Sensei. "Not even the littlest, tiniest bit."

Deja raised her eyebrows in surprise. "Really?" she asked.

"Believe it, young Deja," Sensei replied. "I am as happy as could be. Now that I am no longer gardening, I have so much more time to help other Midlandians."

Sensei turned to Wilda. "In fact," he told her, "I have a great idea for our hurt little friend here."

Wilda sighed. She did not seem to be enjoying

Sensei's help.

"I think it would really cheer this alligator up if we bought him a get-well card and a chocolate ice cream cake from Bun's bakery!" said Sensei.

Wilda smirked. "First off, alligators can't read get-well cards—or anything else," she said. "Second, they don't eat chocolate ice cream. They eat bugs and small animals."

"That does not sound like a very good flavor," Sensei replied. "But no matter; I have another great idea."

Chief could tell that Wilda was becoming frustrated. Even the baby alligator had begun to hiss.

"May I speak with you outside, Sensei?" asked Chief.

"Just as soon as I tell Wilda my plan," he said. "Anyway, I know how we could make that dirty swamp area where this alligator lives much more beautiful. I could plant some fern bushes! Fern bushes soak up lots of water. They will dry that swamp right up! Like the great poet Tiberius Wannadogood wrote—"

"Alligators like swamps!" Wilda burst out.

"No, I don't think that was it," said Sensei.

"They like wet ground, and they like mud, too," Wilda said. "So I will not ever, ever let you plant ferns in the swamp! If you try, the alligators will probably bite you on the fingers, and I wouldn't blame them!"

Everyone was shocked by Wilda's outburst. Even Wilda seemed to be. "Excuse me," she said, blushing. "I have to go find a fresh bandage for this alligator."

Chief and the kids led Sensei out of the hospital. "I don't know why Wilda lost her temper," said Sensei.

"I must be honest," Chief told him. "I believe that your following Wilda around was starting to annoy her."

"Nonsense, Chief!" Sensei replied. "How could my advice be a bother to anyone?"

"It bothered Brushy, too," Logan said. "He was complaining to Chief earlier."

Sensei stopped in his tracks. "He was?" he asked.

Chief nodded. "You give wonderful advice when Midlandians need it," he said. "But there is such a thing as giving too much advice. It stops being a help and becomes a nuisance."

"But..." Sensei began. "If I'm not tending to my garden, and not giving Midlandians advice, what else could I do?"

"You could medi... meditate more," Logan

suggested.

Sensei hung his head. "I've tried," he said. "It is just not the same if I am not in my garden."

"Maybe you need a hobby," advised Deja.

"A hobby?" asked Sensei. "But whatever could I do?"

"Perhaps Deja and Logan could help you find something," Chief said.

"Sure we could," Deja said. "Kid Council to the rescue!"

CHAPTER 5

Hunting for Hobbies

It took days for Deja and Logan to find a hobby that Sensei might like. Each different hobby seemed to have some sort of problem with it.

"You could try fishing," Logan had said. "Chief likes to fish."

"No, no, I could never fish," Sensei had replied. "I would not like being caught with a hook or a net. I am sure the fish do not like it much either."

"You could collect rocks," Deja had said. "Or stamps with pictures of puppies on them!"

"No, no, I would not enjoy collecting stamps," Sensei had said. "I would rather have a hobby that gave me exercise or made me use my mind a lot."

Finally, Logan found an answer. "You could try playing a sport!" he suggested. "Soccer is my favorite."

The very next morning, Sensei met Deja and Logan at the soccer field in Playland Park.

"Are you going to teach me to play?" Sensei asked Logan.

"No!" a voice yelled out behind them. "I'll be your teacher!"

Sensei and the kids turned around. It was Coach! Coach was an expert on fitness. He ran Playland Park and watched over all of the games played there. He made sure that everyone played fairly and safely.

"Coach!" said Sensei. "Good to see you, old friend!"

"Who are you calling old, mister?" Coach replied with a laugh. He jogged over to meet Sensei and the kids, kicking up bits of dirt with his soccer cleats. He was dribbling a soccer ball as he jogged.

"Sensei and I go back a long way," Coach told Deja and Logan. "He was actually the Midlandian who first got me interested in being fit!"

"I didn't know that," Deja said.

"It's true," Sensei agreed. "It was back when Coach was about your age."

"Believe it or not, I was not always this perfect specimen of fitness and health," Coach said. "When I was young, I was very clumsy. I was always tripping over my shoelaces or losing my balance. It made me very embarrassed. I stayed inside a lot and kept to myself."

"I noticed that Coach did not spend much time enjoying the sun or playing with friends," said

Sensei. "So I helped him."

"How did you help?" asked Deja.

"Sensei taught me how to ride a bike!" Coach said. "He helped me learn to keep my balance. He also gave me the confidence to try playing sports. And look at me now!"

Sensei seemed embarrassed. "It was nothing!" he said. "I just showed you what my favorite poet, Stirrspeare Wannadogood, wrote long ago."

Sensei stood up straight and said with a very dramatic voice, "*Stand ye tall, uphold thy duty. A balanced life is a thing of beauty.*"

The kids clapped. "That was like one of Broadway's plays!" Deja said. Broadway was a Midlandian who put on plays and musicals for the whole town.

Coach raised one of his eyebrows. "I don't know much about plays and poems," he said. "But I do know one thing—you taught me balance, and I can't wait to teach you soccer."

"I am always ready to learn," said Sensei.

Coach walked over to the tall, metal goalpost at the field's edge. "The object of the game is to kick the ball through the other team's goal," Coach said. He knocked on the goalpost with his knuckles and it made a ringing sound.

"That is the whole game?" asked Sensei.

"It sounds simple," Coach said. "But each team has a player who protects the goal. That player is the goalie. Goalies are special because they can use their hands to grab the ball. They need very quick reflexes to... think fast!"

In a flash, Coach threw the ball toward Sensei with all of his might. But Sensei was even faster than Coach. His arms shot out and he caught the ball almost too quickly to see it.

"Whoa!" Deja said.

"Just as I thought," Coach said. "Sensei, you're a natural goalie!"

"That was no big deal," said Sensei modestly. "If you really want to surprise me, you should not say 'think fast' before you throw."

"Either way, you made a great stop," Coach said. "In fact, how would you like to join the team I coach for a game tomorrow? You can play goalie for my team, the Stingers."

"That sounds like great fun," said Sensei.

"Congratulations, Sensei," Logan said.

"Brick and Team Laser won't have a chance once I've trained you!" Coach told Sensei. "You kids might want to go find something to do to keep busy. We'll be practicing for quite a while."

Logan and Deja decided to go check on Antigua at the dig site. As they trotted into Sensei's garden, they found Antigua watering the one shrub that she and Venture had not dug up.

Venture was lying on his tummy near the dig. On the ground next to him was a large piece of white paper.

"Animal… is… prehistoric," Venture said as he wrote on the paper.

"What are you doing?" asked Logan.

"We're charting our path to worldwide fame!" Venture said.

"Um… what does that mean?" asked Deja.

"Well, Venture is partly right," said Antigua. "We are making a chart."

"What's the chart for?" asked Logan.

Antigua set down the watering can. "We've found many more bones over the past few days," she said. "But, we are still unsure what kind of animal bones we have dug up. We are making a chart of the facts that we know so far to help us."

Venture hopped to his feet and pointed to the chart. "For example, we know that the bones are fossils," he said.

"A fossil is an object that has been preserved over a long period of time," Antigua explained.

"Also," Venture continued, "these bones are prehistoric. That means that they are older than even the very first history book. They might have come from a dinosaur!"

"That would be so cool," Deja said.

"We know that the bones are hollow," said Antigua. "The animal had a long neck, two legs... and then there are these long bones that we found. They are a bit of a puzzle. They might be arm bones, but we aren't sure. They're awfully long."

Deja lay down near the bones. "You're right," she said. "They're longer than me!"

Suddenly, Logan raised his hand and waved it. "Ooh, I know! Pick me, pick me!" he said.

Antigua laughed. "We're all friends here, Logan, remember?" she said. "You don't need to raise your hand."

Logan dropped his hand. "They're wing bones!" he said.

"Wings?" asked Venture. "What makes you say that?"

"Brushy said that birds have hollow bones to help them fly," he said. "This animal had hollow bones, so maybe it flew, too!"

"You might be onto something here," said Antigua.

"Onto something?" Venture cried. "You might have found the key to unlock this whole animal mystery! I'm going back to the library. I won't leave this time until I've found our flying animal!"

Venture sprinted off, leaving his lunchbox behind.

"He's a little weird," Deja said.

"You have no idea," Antigua replied.

CHAPTER 6

One Coach Too Many

The next day, Deja and Logan went back to Playland Park to watch Sensei play soccer. Coach had chosen Sensei to play goalie for his team, the Stingers.

The Stingers were playing against Team Laser. Team Laser was led by their star player, Brick O. Bobo. Brick was a construction worker, as well as a strong and fast athlete.

Logan and Deja waited on the sidelines for the teams to arrive.

"I can't wait to use my camera at the game!" Logan said.

"I'm just happy that Sensei found a new hobby," Deja said. She had been feeling bad for Sensei ever since Antigua had turned his garden into her latest dig site.

After a little while, the teams came out to play. The Lasers were wearing red uniforms. The Stingers were wearing black and yellow stripes.

The kids watched Coach run onto the field with all of the other Stingers behind him. Finally, they saw Sensei in the back of the crowd.

"There he is!" Deja said. "He looks so cool in

that uniform."

Sensei's uniform was a little different from the other Stingers. His uniform was all yellow instead of striped. Logan snapped a picture of Sensei as he ran toward his goal.

"Let's talk with him before the game starts," Deja said.

When Deja and Logan reached the goalposts, Coach was giving Sensei a pep talk.

"Remember to watch out for Brick," Coach said. "He's the Lasers' best player, and he has a very strong kick." Coach went off to the sidelines.

"How are you feeling?" Deja asked Sensei.

"I am very excited," Sensei replied. "I think soccer will be a great hobby. Thank you both for helping me find it!"

"Do you mind if we stay back here and take pictures?" asked Logan.

"That would be nice," said Sensei. Coach blew his whistle. "Oh, the game is beginning!"

The players on both teams kicked and passed up and down the field. Stingers in stripes flew past Lasers in red. The Lasers stole the ball and shot right back in the other direction. But nobody could make it all the way to the other team's goal.

"If this keeps up," Logan told Sensei, "you'll never even get to make a save!"

But then, one of the Lasers passed the ball to Brick.

"Uh oh," Deja said.

Brick ran circles around the Stingers, kicking the ball as he went. Soon, Sensei was the only Midlandian between Brick and the goal.

Sensei watched Brick approach. When he was just a few feet away from Sensei, Brick kicked the ball with all his might.

With lightning quick hands, Sensei stopped the ball.

"Great save!" Coach shouted from the sidelines.

Sensei was a soccer superstar!

"Don't feel bad," Sensei told Brick as he held the ball. "That was a great kick. But let me give you some advice."

Sensei pointed toward the top corner of the goal. "If you really want a chance to score on me," he said, "try to kick the ball high up into this corner. It is very hard for me to reach there."

"Thanks..." Brick said, a bit confused.

Coach loudly blew his whistle. "Time out!" he shouted. He sprinted over to Sensei's goal.

"Is something the matter?" asked Sensei.

Coach was red with anger. "Brick is not on your team," he hissed. "Why would you tell him how to score goals on you?"

"I stopped his kick so easily," said Sensei. "Now that he knows where to kick, it will be a better challenge for me. It will make playing more fun for both of us."

"You're not out here to have fun!" Coach barked. "You're here to win!"

"With respect, Coach, I must disagree," said Sensei. "Having a good time is more important than winning."

Coach took a deep breath. "You are right about that," he said, but Logan thought it sounded like Coach did not believe what he was saying.

"Just... remember which team you're playing for!" Coach growled. He hustled back to the sidelines.

Logan stepped in toward Sensei. "You're right about having fun," he told Sensei. "My soccer coach said the same thing after we lost a game once. Then he took us out for ice cream."

Sensei smiled. He turned to say something to Logan, but then Coach blew his whistle.

"Game on!" Coach shouted.

Sensei kicked the ball back into play. The Stingers and the Lasers passed the ball up and down the field, left, right, and center. But soon enough, Brick had the ball again.

Sensei watched Brick run toward him very

closely.

"He's going to kick it up into the corner of the goal!" Deja predicted.

Sure enough, Brick launched the ball up into the corner. Sensei leaped up with outstretched fingers. His fingers touched the ball, but it was just too high to grab. Sensei landed on the ground and the soccer ball went through the goal.

"Goal!" Brick shouted.

Brick and his Laser teammates all shouted and gave each other high fives.

Deja saw the frowns of all of the Stingers on the field. "Everyone on Sensei's team looks so disappointed," she said.

"I hope Sensei isn't too upset," Logan said.

But Sensei did not seem bothered at all. In fact, as he dusted the dirt off of his knees, Sensei was laughing!

"That was a great kick!" Sensei told Brick. "I almost had it, too. I can't wait until you kick another high one so that I can try my luck again."

Just before Sensei could shake Brick's hand, Coach's whistle blew again.

"No talking with the other team!" Coach shouted as he ran over. "No talking with the other team! They are the enemy!"

"They are not the enemy, Coach," Sensei

replied. "We might be playing against Team Laser, but they are still our friends. And we could not have such great fun playing without them! That reminds me. I know a terrific Midlandian poem about interdependence."

As Sensei recited the poem, Logan watched Coach grow madder and madder. "His face matches the Lasers' uniforms!" he whispered.

Sensei continued to share the poem without noticing Coach's expression. "*Share a shake of the hand, a tip of the cap, for we are all teammates, from the first to last lap.*"

"Enough!" Coach hollered. "No more poems! Nobody likes hearing your moldy poetry! I'm taking you out of the game."

Deja and Logan were stunned.

"You'd better find another hobby," Coach said. "I need a goalie who wants to win."

CHAPTER 7

Found and Lost

Sensei walked slowly toward the town square. Deja and Logan followed quietly behind him. After Coach had kicked Sensei off of his soccer team, the kids did not know what to say.

As the three reached the town square, Sensei stopped and faced the kids.

"My poems don't annoy you, do they?" he asked.

"I like them," Logan answered.

"I like them, too," Deja said. "I think Coach was wrong to get mad at you. You were just having fun and being a good sport."

"He called my poetry 'moldy,'" said Sensei with a frown.

"I didn't understand that," Logan said. "How can poems have mold on them?"

"If you wrote one on a really big piece of bread it could get moldy," Deja suggested.

"No, no. Coach did not mean that my poems actually had mold on them," Sensei explained. "He just meant that they were old. Actually, it was a very poetic way to say that."

"So Coach is a poet!" Logan said.

"And he didn't even know it," Deja added. Logan and Deja laughed and Sensei joined in.

"You two know how to cheer a Midlandian up," said Sensei. "I needed that. I just have not felt like myself since my garden got dug up."

"But why?" asked Logan.

"It is hard to explain," Sensei replied. "My garden was my home. No, it was so much more than that. I spent many years raising it from a heap of dirt into the most beautiful place in Midlandia. And now...."

Sensei rubbed his forehead. "And now it's just a heap of dirt again," he said. "There is only one lonely, little shrub left. It makes me very sad to think about it."

Deja patted Sensei on the back. "Hey, remember when I was all nervous about breaking my dad's radio?" she asked.

"Of course," Sensei replied.

"You told me a poem and it helped me feel better," Deja said. "Maybe if you found the right poem for yourself, you would feel better about your garden."

"I have thought of every poem that I know, but none of them have helped," said Sensei. "It is very strange. I seem to have ideas and answers for everyone else's problems, but none for my own!"

Logan spotted the Midlandia Library, which stood in the town square. "Maybe you could find some new poems in there," he offered.

"That is a very wise suggestion," said Sensei. "Perhaps my poems are a little moldy. I could use a few fresh ones."

Deja and Logan followed Sensei to the library.

Inside, the three friends found Dewey, the librarian, sitting at his desk. He was in the middle of a game of checkers. Strangely enough, Dewey seemed to be playing alone.

"What are you doing?" Logan asked him.

Dewey looked up. "Oh, hi, everyone!" he said. "I'm just practicing my checkers skills. It's my favorite hobby—but it's better with two players.

Care for a game, Sensei?"

"Not today, my good Midlandian," Sensei replied. "I'd like some help finding a few new books of poetry."

Dewey pushed aside his checkerboard. "I can try," he said. "But I thought you'd already read every poem in this library."

"Gosh, I hope not," said Sensei.

Dewey walked down the aisles with Sensei and the kids behind him. From time to time, Dewey would pull out a poetry book and read its title and author.

"*Summer Sunrise*, by Racquetson Wannadogood," Dewey said.

"I've read it," Sensei replied.

After a while, Dewey had taken Sensei through the entire library. They had not found a single poem that Sensei had not already read.

"I have read every poem in Midlandia," said Sensei with disappointment.

"Are you all right?" asked Deja.

Sensei hung his head. "I think I need to go for a walk," he said.

"Do you want us to come?" asked Logan.

"No, thanks," said Sensei. "I should just walk on my own." He left the children in the library.

"He'll be okay," Dewey promised Deja and

Logan. "Sensei is very wise and very strong. Besides, there is someone else in the library that you might want to see!"

Dewey pointed to a table near the back of the library. There, Deja saw a familiar face.

"It's Venture!" she said.

At his table, Venture was flipping through a very large book. Deja and Logan walked over to visit him.

"How's it going?" asked Deja.

Venture looked up with excitement. "I feel stupendous!" he said. "I am very close to finding our mystery flying animal!"

"Really?" asked Logan. "Was I right? Was it a bird?"

"Actually, I do not believe our animal was a bird," Venture said. "I think it was a kind of flying lizard called a pterosaur."

"I didn't know that lizards could fly," Deja said.

Venture nodded. "Interesting, isn't it?" he said. "There were several kinds of pterosaurs. I've learned a great deal about their wings, which controlled their speed, motion, and movement.

"But there is one missing piece of the puzzle," Venture added.

"What's missing?" asked Logan.

"The skull!" Venture cried. "Antigua still has

not found the animal's skull. You see, most of the bones of each kind of pterosaur are fairly alike. But each kind's skull is different. Look!"

He showed Deja and Logan pictures of different pterosaurs' skulls. Some had very long beaks, while others had points on top.

"Each skull has unique features," Venture explained. "So when we find the skull—"

"You can figure out which animal you've dug up!" Deja deduced.

"Way to put together the pieces, Deja!" Venture said. Then, his tummy made a loud gurgling noise.

Deja giggled. "Was that you?" she asked.

Venture seemed a little embarrassed. "I forgot to pack a lunch," he explained. "Antigua was supposed to bring a sandwich by with my lunchbox, but she must have forgotten. Can you stop by the dig site at Sensei's garden and see if she has my food?"

"No problem," Logan said.

Deja and Logan made the long walk up the Midlandia Trails to Sensei's garden.

Just as they reached the garden, Antigua climbed out of the dig hole. She had what appeared to be a long rock in her hands. She looked more excited than the kids had ever seen her. "Eureka!" she shouted.

As she jumped up and down for joy, the kids rushed over.

"Hey, you two!" said Antigua. "You'll never guess what I found!"

Logan squinted at the object in Antigua's hands. "Is that the skull?" he asked.

Antigua's grin became a smirk. "Well, that's no fun!" she said. "You got it in one guess!"

Logan looked startled. "Oh... sorry," he said.

Antigua laughed. "I'm just kidding, pal," she said. "I'm proud that you guessed correctly. This is a great find! We now have the complete skeleton."

"And you'll be able to figure out which animal these bones came from!" Deja said.

"That's right," said Antigua. "I have to tell Venture!"

"And Sensei," added Logan.

"Yes," Antigua replied. "He'll be excited to get his garden back—even if there is just one shrub left."

Antigua stopped and stood still. She turned around.

"Where did it..." she trailed off.

"What's wrong?" asked Deja.

"Sensei's shrub!" said Antigua. She pointed to a small hole near the dig. "Someone took it!"

CHAPTER 8

Answers for All

Deja and Logan had a brand new mystery on their hands. While Antigua had been at work deep in her dig, someone had come along and plucked Sensei's last remaining shrub from the ground.

The kids could not find Sensei, so they brought Chief Tatupu to the garden to help them.

Antigua seemed heartbroken. "I can't believe I let Sensei down like this," she said. "The shrub was there when I started digging today. I watered it and everything! Someone sneaked in and snatched it from right under my nose."

"There, there, Antigua," Chief said. "It is not your fault that someone took the shrub. You go and work with Venture. The kids and I will take it from here."

Antigua trudged off toward the library.

"Who would steal a shrub from Sensei?" Logan wondered.

"I cannot say," Chief replied. "I cannot imagine a Midlandian doing such a mean thing."

"Sensei did make a lot of Midlandians mad at him over the last week," Deja recalled. "There was Brushy, and Coach, and Wilda...."

"It is true that Sensei did have a conflict with each of them," Chief said. "I do not believe that any one of them would steal, though."

"Shouldn't we at least ask?" Deja said.

"I suppose you are right," Chief agreed.

"Before we go..." Logan began. He hurried over to the place where Sensei's shrub had once been planted. He took a picture of the hole in the ground with his digital camera.

"We need this for evidence," he said. "I saw it on TV."

"Anyway..." Deja said. "Should we split up?"

"No, we should stick together this time," Chief said. "Let us start at Brushy's office."

"Someone stole Sensei's shrub?" Brushy said. He looked at the picture Logan had taken. "That's awful!"

Chief was standing with Brushy in his examination room. Deja and Logan sat on stools near Brushy's tool tray and watched.

"I hate to ask this, Brushy," Chief said, "but do you know anything about what happened to it?"

Brushy's jaw dropped. "Why... you can't possibly think that I had something to do with this thievery!" he said.

"We're sorry," Logan said. "But we have to ask everyone who Sensei spent time with this week."

Brushy was stunned. "I'd never... never ever..." he stammered. He took a deep breath. "Sensei made me mad when he messed up my golden pheasant picture, but I would never steal from him. I believe in forgiveness and cooperation. I don't hold grudges."

"Thanks for talking with us, Brushy," Deja said.

After they left Brushy's office, Chief brought Deja and Logan to Playland Park.

Coach was umpiring a softball game when they arrived. At the end of the inning, Coach stepped aside to talk for a few minutes.

"Let's keep it friendly, folks!" Coach told both softball teams. He turned to face Chief and the kids. "What can I do for you?"

Chief explained how Sensei's shrub had gone missing. As Chief spoke, Coach took off his ball cap and held it in his hands.

"This is just not a good day for Sensei," Coach said. "I am so embarrassed about how I treated him earlier."

The kids were surprised. "You are?" asked Logan.

Coach looked at his sneakers. "After I cooled off, I realized that Sensei was just showing good sportsmanship," he said meekly. "He was right, and I was wrong. Competition is important in sports, but it isn't everything. I set a lousy example for you youngsters."

"So you don't know anything about Sensei's shrub disappearing?" asked Deja.

"No, ma'am!" Coach said.

Deja grinned and her braces shined. "He called me *ma'am*," she whispered to Logan.

"I was right here at the park all day," Coach said. "But when you find the culprit, send him my way. I'll make that lowdown scoundrel run laps until his legs turn to jelly!"

With Coach out of the picture, there was only one Midlandian left for Chief and the kids to speak with: Wilda. Logan opened the doors to the conservation center. Deja and Chief followed him in.

Deja froze in her tracks. "Hold it!" she said. Logan and Chief stopped.

Deja pointed to the ground. There was a thin trail of dirt leading from the door to the hallway. "That might be a clue," she noted.

"Oh, cool," Logan said. He knelt on the floor and took a picture of the dirt. "Let's follow the trail!"

The trio did as Logan suggested. After a short distance, the trail turned left and stopped at a doorway.

"It leads into the animal hospital," Chief said. "I cannot believe it. It really seems like Wilda took Sensei's shrub."

"Let's go in," Deja said.

Chief pushed open the door to the animal hospital.

Inside, Wilda was not alone.

"Sensei?" Logan said.

Wilda was wrapping a bandage around Sensei's hand. Sensei's shrub was lying on the floor next to his feet.

"Hello, everyone," said Sensei.

"You found your shrub!" Chief declared.

Sensei raised his eyebrow. "Of course I did," he said. "It was in my garden, after all."

"I am confused," Chief said. "Do you mean that you dug up your own shrub?"

"And then he tried to plant it in Animal Land," Wilda said.

"Sensei!" Deja cried. "Did you get bitten by an alligator?"

Sensei shook his head. "No, I stayed away from the swamp," he replied. "Wilda said it was dangerous. I went to the deciduous forest."

Wilda shook her head with a smile. "And so he got scratched by a bird instead," she told them. "I brought the bird in, too. He's in a cage near the corner."

Logan looked at the bird. It had blue wings, but the feathers near its crown and tail were gold.

"It's the golden pheasant!" he exclaimed. He took a few pictures of the bird.

"I've learned my lesson," said Sensei. "I should not intrude on another animal's habitat, whether it's a lizard, a bird, or anything in between."

"Why did you bring your shrub here in the first place?" Deja asked him.

"I got so sad that there were no more poems for me to read," Sensei replied. "I didn't know what to do. So I thought I'd try the only other thing that makes me feel great, which is gardening."

Sensei held up his bandaged hand. "It was not a wise decision, as you can see," he said.

"But Sensei," Deja said, "if there were no more poems at the library, why didn't you just write some new ones?"

Sensei looked at her for a long time.

"Um..." Deja began. "I don't have anything stuck in my braces, do I?"

"Not a morsel," said Sensei. "I am just astounded

by your wisdom!"

"What's a stounded?" asked Deja.

"No, no, the word *astounded* means amazed," said Sensei. "The answer seems so simple now."

Logan leaned in toward Chief. "What is he talking about?" he whispered.

"It is so clear what my hobby should be," said Sensei.

"I have become wise by reading the great poets of Midlandia," he went on. "Perhaps if I work very hard, I can be Midlandia's next great poet! Thank you so much, Deja."

"Me?" she replied.

"Ever since my garden got dug up," Sensei explained, "it has been as if part of me had been taken away. But now," he said with a huge smile, "you have helped me find the way to put myself together again!"

CHAPTER 9

Midlandia's Newest Poet

Deja and Logan did not see much of Sensei for the next few weeks. He had locked himself away to write some new poems for the Midlandians to enjoy.

Deja and Logan did not see much of Antigua or Venture, either. They were busy cleaning the skeleton they had dug up and fitting the bones together.

Instead, the kids hung out with Coach. He and Logan spent the time teaching Deja about soccer.

"Dribble with the left, fake to the right," Coach said. "And... shoot!"

Deja kicked the soccer ball toward the goal. Logan tried to stop the ball, but it rolled through the goalposts and hit the net behind him.

"Wow, nice kick," Logan said.

"You made a good try, too," Coach told Logan. "Maybe the two of you could sub in the next time my Stingers have a game!"

Deja and Logan looked at each other. "Um..."

Deja began.

"We'll see," Logan said.

At that moment, Posta, the mail carrier, approached the field on her special mail bike. It had a sidecar that she used to carry letters, packages, and sometimes other Midlandians who were in a hurry.

"No riding on the field!" Coach bellowed.

"I know, I know," Posta said. She parked her bike along the sidelines. "I have a letter for you."

She handed a small envelope to Coach and then rode off on her bike.

Coach opened the envelope and read the note inside. "It's an invitation!" he said.

"Is it for a concert?" asked Logan.

"Or an ice cream party?" hoped Deja.

"Nope," Coach replied. "Here is what it says:

"'Doctors Antigua O. Bobo and Venture Wannadogood proudly invite you to the Midlandia Museum of Natural History for the unveiling of their latest discovery.'"

"That must be the skeleton!" Deja said.

"Does it say what kind of animal it is?" asked Logan.

"No... I guess they're saving that for the ceremony," Coach said. "But there is more. Listen:

"'With special guest Sensei Wannadogood

reading his brand new poem!'" he read.

"That's awesome," Logan said. "We can't miss it. When is it happening?"

"This afternoon!" Coach said. "I'd better put away these shin pads and dig out my tux."

When Deja and Logan arrived at the museum, the main hall was packed.

"So many Midlandians came!" Deja said, as they squeezed through the crowd.

Logan squinted through his glasses. He saw Venture and Antigua standing next to a large object that was hanging from ropes and pulleys. The object was covered with a cloth.

"I'll bet the skeleton is under there!" Logan guessed. "But where's Sensei?"

"I think I see him over near the corner!" Deja said.

Sensei stood on the other side of the room. He looked happier than the kids had seen him in weeks. He was speaking with Wilda, who was holding a small, potted plant.

The kids inched their way through the crowd. Eventually, they made it to Sensei.

"Thanks again for the lovely gift!" Wilda said.

"You can keep it in your office, far away from the wild animals," Sensei told her.

As Wilda moved on, Coach squeezed in next to
Sensei. Coach was wearing a black tuxedo with
tails that nearly reached the ground.

"Did I overdress?" asked Coach.

"You look great, old friend," said Sensei with a
laugh.

"Can you forgive me for being such a grouch
during the soccer game?" asked Coach.

"Of course," said Sensei. "In fact, I have a small
gift for you as well."

Sensei pulled a pair of gloves from his pocket
and handed them to Coach.

"I had Sew the seamstress stitch some letters
on them," Sensei noted.

Coach put on the gloves. On one hand was the
word "team." On the other hand was the word
"work."

"Now hold your hands together," said Sensei.

Coach put his hands next to each other.
"Teamwork!" he said. "What a great present,
Sensei. Thanks! And good luck with your new
poem!"

Coach moved on.

"That was a cool idea," Logan told Sensei.

"Oh, greetings, my young friends!" said Sensei.

"Sensei! Oh, Sensei!" a voice called.

"I recognize that voice," Deja said. It was

Brushy. He was weaving through the crowd toward Sensei.

"I would like to apologize for bothering you before," Sensei told Brushy.

"Oh, don't trouble yourself, Sensei," Brushy replied.

"I have something for you," said Sensei. He took a small picture frame from his pocket.

"Sensei!" Brushy cried, holding the picture. "It's a picture of the golden pheasant!"

"Logan took the picture," Sensei explained. "But he gave me a copy to frame for you."

"Thanks, you two!" Brushy said. "This is going up in my office, right next to the x-ray machine!"

"You sure gave out a lot of presents," Deja said.

"I still have one more to share," Sensei replied.

"What is it?" Deja asked.

Before Sensei could answer, Venture cleared his throat loudly.

"Everyone!" Venture shouted. "May I have your attention?"

The crowd quieted down and became still.

"Antigua and I thank you all for coming!" Venture said. "I want there to be plenty of time for interviews, so I will keep this brief.

"Some weeks ago," he continued, "Antigua and I began digging up some mysterious bones in

Sensei's garden. Soon, with the help of the Kid Council, we realized that these were no ordinary fossils, but the bones of an ancient and rare flying creature. And here it is! We present to you... the pteranodon!"

"So that's what it's called!" Logan said to Deja.

Venture pulled down the sheet covering the skeleton. It was posed as if it were flying. The whole crowd burst into applause.

As the clapping died down, Venture spoke up again. "Antigua and I will be taking interviews shortly," he said. "But first, a poem from our good friend Sensei!"

Everyone clapped as Sensei moved toward the hanging skeleton.

"You are too kind," Sensei told the crowd. "This is my first poem, but I hope it is the first of many. I dedicate it to my friends Deja and Logan."

Sensei looked right at the pair. "Without you two, I would never have written this," he said. "Think of it as my gift to you.

"My poem is called 'Second Chances,'" Sensei said. He began to read.

"*The land was his, before it was mine.*
Locked away in rock for all time.
With picks, brushes, and curiosity
His bones, at long last, were set free.

But what great cost!
My garden, lost.
And like it, so was I.
But from the corner of my eye
I saw a splash of color bloom;
A yellow rose, amid the gloom!
The garden grew,
So fresh and new,
Reaching toward the sky.
And like it, so will I."'

The applause from the crowd was like thunder. But no one clapped louder than Deja and Logan.

Sensei took a small bow and winked at his two young friends. Then Midlandia's newest poet moved away from the skeleton and joined the pair to celebrate with a glass of blueberry punch.

Discussion Questions

In the book, Sensei has trouble dealing with the sudden change of losing his garden. Have you ever had a difficult change in your life? How did you handle it?

Early in the book, Deja does not want to tell her father about breaking his radio. Why is it best not to keep secrets? Have you ever kept a secret? What happened?

For a while, Sensei becomes a nuisance to the other Midlandians. How does he bother them? Why does he do it?

There are many examples of different hobbies that appear throughout the story. Do any of those hobbies interest you? Which ones? Do you have anything in common with the characters who enjoyed these hobbies?

Sensei finds an outlet for his troubles by writing poetry. What other creative ways could he have expressed himself? Was poetry the best choice for Sensei? Why?